# The Dream Team

Written by Jane Langford

Illustrated by John Eastwood

Wayne's dad was a dreamer.
In the day, he drove a truck.
At night, he dreamed of being
a soccer coach.

He often joked about it.

"One day my soccer team will win the World Cup!" he told Wayne.

Wayne put his fingers in his ears.
"Stop him talking like that, Mom!"
he said. "Dad's a truck driver, not a
soccer coach!"

Mom looked at Wayne.
"There's nothing wrong with
dreaming," she said.

One day, Wayne's friends came over. Wayne's dad came in.

"When I am the coach of my soccer team, I'll call it the Dream Team," he told them.

"Wow," gasped Wayne's friends.
"Are you a soccer coach?"
Wayne's face turned red.
"No, he's not!" he shouted.
"He's a truck driver!"

Wayne's dad looked upset.
After that, he stopped talking about
being a soccer coach. He stopped
talking about his Dream Team.

Wayne missed all the soccer talk.
He missed his dad's happy smile.

"Tell me about the Dream Team,"
he said.

But Dad said, "Nothing to tell."

"I wish I hadn't shouted at Dad,"
said Wayne. "What can I do?"

"Nothing," said Mom. "He's lost his
dream. How can we cheer him up?"

Wayne thought.

"I've got an idea," he said.

The next day Wayne had a long talk with his teacher. That night the doorbell rang. It was Mr. Beamer from school.

"Hello," he said. "Wayne tells me
you'd like to be a soccer coach."
Dad's face turned red.

"Er — yes," he said. "I would."

"Well," said Mr. Beamer. "would you
like to coach our beginner's team?
It won't be easy. They're not very
good, but they do want to be
the best team in the world!"

"I've talked about being a soccer coach," said Dad. "It's about time I tried it. Yes, I'll do it!"
He gave Wayne a hug.

"My very own Dream Team!" he said.